Robert Louis Stevenson (13 November 1850 – 3 December 1894) was a Scottish novelist and travel writer, most noted for Treasure Island, Kidnapped, Strange Case of Dr Jekyll and Mr Hyde, and A Child's Garden of Verses. Born and educated in Edinburgh, Stevenson suffered from serious bronchial trouble for much of his life, but continued to write prolifically and travel widely, in defiance of his poor health. As a young man, he mixed in London literary circles, receiving encouragement from Andrew Lang, Edmund Gosse, Leslie Stephen and W. E. Henley, the last of whom may have provided the model for Long John Silver in Treasure Island. His travels took him to France, America and Australia, before he finally settled in Samoa, where he died. A celebrity in his lifetime, Stevenson attracted a more negative critical response for much of the 20th century, though his reputation has been largely restored. He is currently ranked as the 26th most translated author in the world.(Source: Wikipedia)

Literary works:
The Hair Trunk or
The Ideal Commonwealth (1877)
Treasure Island (1883)
Prince Otto (1885)
Strange Case of Dr Jekyll and Mr Hyde (1886),
Kidnapped (1886)
The Black Arrow: A Tale of the Two Roses (1888)
The Master of Ballantrae: A Winter's Tale (1889),
The Wrong Box (1889)
The Wrecker (1892); co-written with Lloyd Osbourne.
Catriona (1893)
The Ebb-Tide (1894); co-written with Lloyd Osbourne.
Weir of Hermiston (1896)
St-Ives: Being the Adventures of a
French Prisoner in England (1897)

UNDERWOODS
ROBERT LOUIS STEVENSON

PRINCE CLASSICS

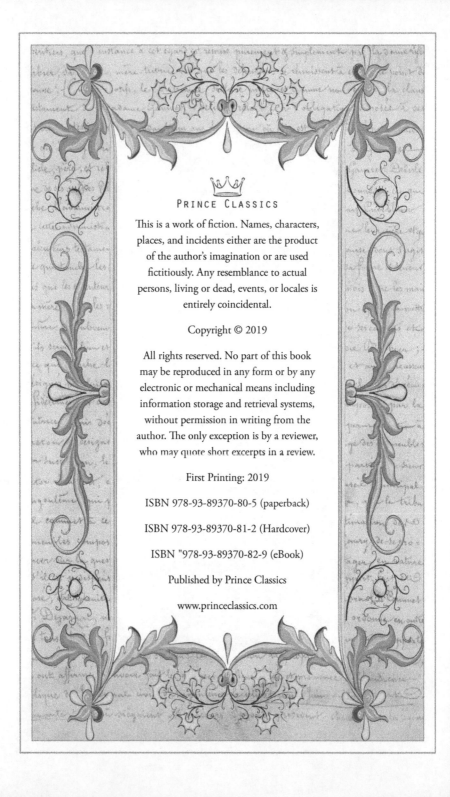

PRINCE CLASSICS

This is a work of fiction. Names, characters, places, and incidents either are the product of the author's imagination or are used fictitiously. Any resemblance to actual persons, living or dead, events, or locales is entirely coincidental.

Copyright © 2019

All rights reserved. No part of this book may be reproduced in any form or by any electronic or mechanical means including information storage and retrieval systems, without permission in writing from the author. The only exception is by a reviewer, who may quote short excerpts in a review.

First Printing: 2019

ISBN 978-93-89370-80-5 (paperback)

ISBN 978-93-89370-81-2 (Hardcover)

ISBN "978-93-89370-82-9 (eBook)

Published by Prince Classics

www.princeclassics.com

Contents

DEDICATION	12
NOTE	14
BOOK I.—In English	**17**
I—ENVOY	17
II—A SONG OF THE ROAD	17
III—THE CANOE SPEAKS	19
IV	20
V—THE HOUSE BEAUTIFUL	22
VI—A VISIT FROM THE SEA	23
VII—TO A GARDENER	24
VIII—TO MINNIE	26
IX—TO K. DE M.	27
X—TO N. V. DE G. S.	28
XI—TO WILL. H. LOW	29
XII—TO MRS. WILL. H. LOW	30
XIII—TO H. F. BROWN	31
XIV—TO ANDREW LANG	33
XV—ET TU IN ARCADIA VIXISTI	34
XVI—TO W. E. HENLEY	38
XVII—HENRY JAMES	39
XVIII—THE MIRROR SPEAKS	40
XIX—KATHARINE	41
XX—TO F. J. S.	42
XXI—REQUIEM	42
XXII—THE CELESTIAL SURGEON	43
XXIII—OUR LADY OF THE SNOWS	44
XXIV	47
XXV	49
XXVI—THE SICK CHILD	51
XXVII—IN MEMORIAM F. A. S.	52

XXVIII—TO MY FATHER	53
XXIX—IN THE STATES	54
XXX—A PORTRAIT	55
XXXI	56
XXXII—A CAMP [66]	57
XXXIII—THE COUNTRY OF THE CAMISARDS [67]	57
XXXIV—SKERRYVORE	57
XXXV—SKERRYVORE: The Parallel	58
XXXVI	58
XXXVII	59
XXXVIII	60
BOOK II.—In Scots	**62**
TABLE OF COMMON SCOTTISH VOWEL SOUNDS	62
I—THE MAKER TO POSTERITY	63
II—ILLE TERRARUM	65
III	69
IV—A MILE AN' A BITTOCK	70
V—A LOWDEN SABBATH MORN	71
VI—THE SPAEWIFE	79
VII—THE BLAST—1875	80
VIII—THE COUNTERBLAST—1886	82
IX—THE COUNTERBLAST IRONICAL	85
X—THEIR LAUREATE TO AN ACADEMY CLASS DINNER CLUB	87
XI—EMBRO HIE KIRK	90
XII—THE SCOTSMAN'S RETURN FROM ABROAD	93
XIII	98
XIV—MY CONSCIENCE!	102
XV—TO DOCTOR JOHN BROWN	104
XVI	107
Footnotes	109
About Author	111

UNDERWOODS

Of all my verse, like not a single line;

But like my title, for it is not mine.

That title from a better man I stole:

Ah, how much better, had I stol'n the whole!

DEDICATION

There are men and classes of men that stand above the common herd: the soldier, the sailor and the shepherd not unfrequently; the artist rarely; rarely still, the clergyman; the physician almost as a rule. He is the flower (such as it is) of our civilisation; and when that stage of man is done with, and only remembered to be marvelled at in history, he will be thought to have shared as little as any in the defects of the period, and most notably exhibited the virtues of the race. Generosity he has, such as is possible to those who practise an art, never to those who drive a trade; discretion, tested by a hundred secrets; tact, tried in a thousand embarrassments; and what are more important, Heraclean cheerfulness and courage. So it is that he brings air and cheer into the sickroom, and often enough, though not so often as he wishes, brings healing.

Gratitude is but a lame sentiment; thanks, when they are expressed, are often more embarrassing than welcome; and yet I must set forth mine to a few out of many doctors who have brought me comfort and help: to Dr. Willey of San Francisco, whose kindness to a stranger it must be as grateful to him, as it is touching to me, to remember; to Dr. Karl Ruedi of Davos, the good genius of the English in his frosty mountains; to Dr. Herbert of Paris, whom I knew only for a week, and to Dr. Caissot of Montpellier, whom I knew only for ten days, and who have yet written their names deeply in my memory; to Dr. Brandt of Royat; to Dr. Wakefield of Nice; to Dr. Chepmell, whose visits make it a pleasure to be ill; to Dr. Horace Dobell, so wise in counsel; to Sir Andrew Clark, so unwearied in kindness and to that wise youth, my uncle, Dr. Balfour.

I forget as many as I remember; and I ask both to pardon me, these for silence, those for inadequate speech. But one name I have kept on purpose to the last, because it is a household word with me, and because if I had not received favours from so many hands and in so many quarters of the world, it should have stood upon this page alone: that of my friend Thomas Bodley

Scott of Bournemouth. Will he accept this, although shared among so many, for a dedication to himself? and when next my ill-fortune (which has thus its pleasant side) brings him hurrying to me when he would fain sit down to meat or lie down to rest, will he care to remember that he takes this trouble for one who is not fool enough to be ungrateful?

R. L. S.

Skerryvore,

    Bournemouth.

NOTE

The human conscience has fled of late the troublesome domain of conduct for what I should have supposed to be the less congenial field of art: there she may now be said to rage, and with special severity in all that touches dialect; so that in every novel the letters of the alphabet are tortured, and the reader wearied, to commemorate shades of mis-pronunciation. Now spelling is an art of great difficulty in my eyes, and I am inclined to lean upon the printer, even in common practice, rather than to venture abroad upon new quests. And the Scots tongue has an orthography of its own, lacking neither "authority nor author." Yet the temptation is great to lend a little guidance to the bewildered Englishman. Some simple phonetic artifice might defend your verses from barbarous mishandling, and yet not injure any vested interest. So it seems at first; but there are rocks ahead. Thus, if I wish the diphthong ou to have its proper value, I may write oor instead of our; many have done so and lived, and the pillars of the universe remained unshaken. But if I did so, and came presently to doun, which is the classical Scots spelling of the English down, I should begin to feel uneasy; and if I went on a little farther, and came to a classical Scots word, like stour or dour or clour, I should know precisely where I was—that is to say, that I was out of sight of land on those high seas of spelling reform in which so many strong swimmers have toiled vainly. To some the situation is exhilarating; as for me, I give one bubbling cry and sink. The compromise at which I have arrived is indefensible, and I have no thought of trying to defend it. As I have stuck for the most part to the proper spelling, I append a table of some common vowel sounds which no one need consult; and just to prove that I belong to my age and have in me the stuff of a reformer, I have used modification marks throughout. Thus I can tell myself, not without pride, that I have added a fresh stumbling-block for English readers, and to a page of print in my native tongue, have lent a new uncouthness. Sed non nobis.

I note again, that among our new dialecticians, the local habitat of every dialect is given to the square mile. I could not emulate this nicety if I desired;

for I simply wrote my Scots as well as I was able, not caring if it hailed from Lauderdale or Angus, from the Mearns or Galloway; if I had ever heard a good word, I used it without shame; and when Scots was lacking, or the rhyme jibbed, I was glad (like my betters) to fall back on English. For all that, I own to a friendly feeling for the tongue of Fergusson and of Sir Walter, both Edinburgh men; and I confess that Burns has always sounded in my ear like something partly foreign. And indeed I am from the Lothians myself; it is there I heard the language spoken about my childhood; and it is in the drawling Lothian voice that I repeat it to myself. Let the precisians call my speech that of the Lothians. And if it be not pure, alas! what matters it? The day draws near when this illustrious and malleable tongue shall be quite forgotten; and Burn's Ayrshire, and Dr. Macdonald's Aberdeen-awa', and Scott's brave, metropolitan utterance will be all equally the ghosts of speech. Till then I would love to have my hour as a native Maker, and be read by my own countryfolk in our own dying language: an ambition surely rather of the heart than of the head, so restricted as it is in prospect of endurance, so parochial in bounds of space.

BOOK I.—In English

I—ENVOY

Go, little book, and wish to all

Flowers in the garden, meat in the hall,

A bin of wine, a spice of wit,

A house with lawns enclosing it,

A living river by the door,

A nightingale in the sycamore!

II—A SONG OF THE ROAD

The gauger walked with willing foot,

And aye the gauger played the flute;

And what should Master Gauger play

But *Over the hills and far away?*

Whene'er I buckle on my pack

And foot it gaily in the track,

O pleasant gauger, long since dead,

I hear you fluting on ahead.

You go with me the self-same way—

The self-same air for me you play;
For I do think and so do you
It is the tune to travel to.

For who would gravely set his face
To go to this or t'other place?
There's nothing under Heav'n so blue
That's fairly worth the travelling to.

On every hand the roads begin,
And people walk with zeal therein;
But wheresoe'er the highways tend,
Be sure there's nothing at the end.

Then follow you, wherever hie
The travelling mountains of the sky.
Or let the streams in civil mode
Direct your choice upon a road;

For one and all, or high or low,
Will lead you where you wish to go;
And one and all go night and day
Over the hills and far away!

Forest of Montargis, 1878.

III—THE CANOE SPEAKS

On the great streams the ships may go

About men's business to and fro.

But I, the egg-shell pinnace, sleep

On crystal waters ankle-deep:

I, whose diminutive design,

Of sweeter cedar, pithier pine,

Is fashioned on so frail a mould,

A hand may launch, a hand withhold:

I, rather, with the leaping trout

Wind, among lilies, in and out;

I, the unnamed, inviolate,

Green, rustic rivers, navigate;

My dipping paddle scarcely shakes

The berry in the bramble-brakes;

Still forth on my green way I wend

Beside the cottage garden-end;

And by the nested angler fare,

And take the lovers unaware.

By willow wood and water-wheel

Speedily fleets my touching keel;

By all retired and shady spots

Where prosper dim forget-me-nots;

By meadows where at afternoon
The growing maidens troop in June
To loose their girdles on the grass.
Ah! speedier than before the glass
The backward toilet goes; and swift
As swallows quiver, robe and shift
And the rough country stockings lie
Around each young divinity.
When, following the recondite brook,
Sudden upon this scene I look,
And light with unfamiliar face
On chaste Diana's bathing-place,
Loud ring the hills about and all
The shallows are abandoned. . . .

IV

It is the season now to go
About the country high and low,
Among the lilacs hand in hand,
And two by two in fairy land.

The brooding boy, the sighing maid,
Wholly fain and half afraid,

Now meet along the hazel'd brook
To pass and linger, pause and look.

A year ago, and blithely paired,
Their rough-and-tumble play they shared;
They kissed and quarrelled, laughed and cried,
A year ago at Eastertide.

With bursting heart, with fiery face,
She strove against him in the race;
He unabashed her garter saw,
That now would touch her skirts with awe.

Now by the stile ablaze she stops,
And his demurer eyes he drops;
Now they exchange averted sighs
Or stand and marry silent eyes.

And he to her a hero is
And sweeter she than primroses;
Their common silence dearer far
Than nightingale and mavis are.

Now when they sever wedded hands,

Joy trembles in their bosom-strands

And lovely laughter leaps and falls

Upon their lips in madrigals.

V—THE HOUSE BEAUTIFUL

A naked house, a naked moor,

A shivering pool before the door,

A garden bare of flowers and fruit

And poplars at the garden foot:

Such is the place that I live in,

Bleak without and bare within.

Yet shall your ragged moor receive

The incomparable pomp of eve,

And the cold glories of the dawn

Behind your shivering trees be drawn;

And when the wind from place to place

Doth the unmoored cloud-galleons chase,

Your garden gloom and gleam again,

With leaping sun, with glancing rain.

Here shall the wizard moon ascend

The heavens, in the crimson end

Of day's declining splendour; here

The army of the stars appear.

The neighbour hollows dry or wet,

Spring shall with tender flowers beset;

And oft the morning muser see

Larks rising from the broomy lea,

And every fairy wheel and thread

Of cobweb dew-bediamonded.

When daisies go, shall winter time

Silver the simple grass with rime;

Autumnal frosts enchant the pool

And make the cart-ruts beautiful;

And when snow-bright the moor expands,

How shall your children clap their hands!

To make this earth our hermitage,

A cheerful and a changeful page,

God's bright and intricate device

Of days and seasons doth suffice.

VI—A VISIT FROM THE SEA

Far from the loud sea beaches
   Where he goes fishing and crying,
Here in the inland garden
   Why is the sea-gull flying?

Here are no fish to dive for;

Here is the corn and lea;
Here are the green trees rustling.
  Hie away home to sea!

Fresh is the river water
  And quiet among the rushes;
This is no home for the sea-gull
  But for the rooks and thrushes.

Pity the bird that has wandered!
  Pity the sailor ashore!
Hurry him home to the ocean,
  Let him come here no more!

High on the sea-cliff ledges
  The white gulls are trooping and crying,
Here among the rooks and roses,
  Why is the sea-gull flying?

VII—TO A GARDENER

Friend, in my mountain-side demesne
My plain-beholding, rosy, green
And linnet-haunted garden-ground,
Let still the esculents abound.

Let first the onion flourish there,

Rose among roots, the maiden-fair,

Wine-scented and poetic soul

Of the capacious salad bowl.

Let thyme the mountaineer (to dress

The tinier birds) and wading cress,

The lover of the shallow brook,

From all my plots and borders look.

Nor crisp and ruddy radish, nor

Pease-cods for the child's pinafore

Be lacking; nor of salad clan

The last and least that ever ran

About great nature's garden-beds.

Nor thence be missed the speary heads

Of artichoke; nor thence the bean

That gathered innocent and green

Outsavours the belauded pea.

These tend, I prithee; and for me,

Thy most long-suffering master, bring

In April, when the linnets sing

And the days lengthen more and more

At sundown to the garden door.

And I, being provided thus.

Shall, with superb asparagus,

A book, a taper, and a cup

Of country wine, divinely sup.

La Solitude, Hyères.

VIII—TO MINNIE

(With a hand-glass)

A picture-frame for you to fill,

    A paltry setting for your face,

A thing that has no worth until

    You lend it something of your grace

I send (unhappy I that sing

    Laid by awhile upon the shelf)

Because I would not send a thing

    Less charming than you are yourself.

And happier than I, alas!

    (Dumb thing, I envy its delight)

'Twill wish you well, the looking-glass,

And look you in the face to-night.

1869.

IX—TO K. DE M.

A lover of the moorland bare

And honest country winds, you were;

The silver-skimming rain you took;

And loved the floodings of the brook,

Dew, frost and mountains, fire and seas,

Tumultuary silences,

Winds that in darkness fifed a tune,

And the high-riding, virgin moon.

And as the berry, pale and sharp,

Springs on some ditch's counterscarp

In our ungenial, native north—

You put your frosted wildings forth,

And on the heath, afar from man,

A strong and bitter virgin ran.

The berry ripened keeps the rude

And racy flavour of the wood.

And you that loved the empty plain

All redolent of wind and rain,
Around you still the curlew sings—
The freshness of the weather clings—
The maiden jewels of the rain
Sit in your dabbled locks again.

X—TO N. V. DE G. S.

The unfathomable sea, and time, and tears,
The deeds of heroes and the crimes of kings
Dispart us; and the river of events
Has, for an age of years, to east and west
More widely borne our cradles. Thou to me
Art foreign, as when seamen at the dawn
Descry a land far off and know not which.
So I approach uncertain; so I cruise
Round thy mysterious islet, and behold
Surf and great mountains and loud river-bars,
And from the shore hear inland voices call.

Strange is the seaman's heart; he hopes, he fears;
Draws closer and sweeps wider from that coast;
Last, his rent sail refits, and to the deep
His shattered prow uncomforted puts back.
Yet as he goes he ponders at the helm

Of that bright island; where he feared to touch,

His spirit readventures; and for years,

Where by his wife he slumbers safe at home,

Thoughts of that land revisit him; he sees

The eternal mountains beckon, and awakes

Yearning for that far home that might have been.

XI—TO WILL. H. LOW

Youth now flees on feathered foot

Faint and fainter sounds the flute,

Rarer songs of gods; and still

Somewhere on the sunny hill,

Or along the winding stream,

Through the willows, flits a dream;

Flits but shows a smiling face,

Flees but with so quaint a grace,

None can choose to stay at home,

All must follow, all must roam.

This is unborn beauty: she

Now in air floats high and free,

Takes the sun and breaks the blue;—

Late with stooping pinion flew

Raking hedgerow trees, and wet

Her wing in silver streams, and set
Shining foot on temple roof:
Now again she flies aloof,
Coasting mountain clouds and kiss't
By the evening's amethyst.

In wet wood and miry lane,
Still we pant and pound in vain;
Still with leaden foot we chase
Waning pinion, fainting face;
Still with gray hair we stumble on,
Till, behold, the vision gone!

Where hath fleeting beauty led?
To the doorway of the dead.
Life is over, life was gay:
We have come the primrose way.

XII—TO MRS. WILL. H. LOW

Even in the bluest noonday of July,
There could not run the smallest breath of wind
But all the quarter sounded like a wood;
And in the chequered silence and above
The hum of city cabs that sought the Bois,

Suburban ashes shivered into song.

A patter and a chatter and a chirp

And a long dying hiss—it was as though

Starched old brocaded dames through all the house

Had trailed a strident skirt, or the whole sky

Even in a wink had over-brimmed in rain.

Hark, in these shady parlours, how it talks

Of the near Autumn, how the smitten ash

Trembles and augurs floods! O not too long

In these inconstant latitudes delay,

O not too late from the unbeloved north

Trim your escape! For soon shall this low roof

Resound indeed with rain, soon shall your eyes

Search the foul garden, search the darkened rooms,

Nor find one jewel but the blazing log.

12 Rue Vernier, Paris.

XIII—TO H. F. BROWN

(Written during a dangerous sickness.)

I sit and wait a pair of oars

On cis-Elysian river-shores.

Where the immortal dead have sate,

'Tis mine to sit and meditate;

To re-ascend life's rivulet,

Without remorse, without regret;

And sing my Alma Genetrix

Among the willows of the Styx.

And lo, as my serener soul

Did these unhappy shores patrol,

And wait with an attentive ear

The coming of the gondolier,

Your fire-surviving roll I took,

Your spirited and happy book; [27]

Whereon, despite my frowning fate,

It did my soul so recreate

That all my fancies fled away

On a Venetian holiday.

Now, thanks to your triumphant care,

Your pages clear as April air,

The sails, the bells, the birds, I know,

And the far-off Friulan snow;

The land and sea, the sun and shade,

And the blue even lamp-inlaid.

For this, for these, for all, O friend,

For your whole book from end to end—

For Paron Piero's muttonham—

I your defaulting debtor am.

Perchance, reviving, yet may I

To your sea-paven city hie,

And in a felze, some day yet

Light at your pipe my cigarette.

XIV—TO ANDREW LANG

Dear Andrew, with the brindled hair,

Who glory to have thrown in air,

High over arm, the trembling reed,

By Ale and Kail, by Till and Tweed:

An equal craft of hand you show

The pen to guide, the fly to throw:

I count you happy starred; for God,

When He with inkpot and with rod

Endowed you, bade your fortune lead

Forever by the crooks of Tweed,

Forever by the woods of song

And lands that to the Muse belong;

Or if in peopled streets, or in

The abhorred pedantic sanhedrim,

It should be yours to wander, still

Airs of the morn, airs of the hill,

The plovery Forest and the seas

That break about the Hebrides,

Should follow over field and plain

And find you at the window pane;

And you again see hill and peel,

And the bright springs gush at your heel.

So went the fiat forth, and so

Garrulous like a brook you go,

With sound of happy mirth and sheen

Of daylight—whether by the green

You fare that moment, or the gray;

Whether you dwell in March or May;

Or whether treat of reels and rods

Or of the old unhappy gods:

Still like a brook your page has shone,

And your ink sings of Helicon.

XV—ET TU IN ARCADIA VIXISTI

(TO R. A. M. S.)

In ancient tales, O friend, thy spirit dwelt;

There, from of old, thy childhood passed; and there

High expectation, high delights and deeds,

Thy fluttering heart with hope and terror moved.

And thou hast heard of yore the Blatant Beast,

And Roland's horn, and that war-scattering shout

Of all-unarmed Achilles, ægis-crowned

And perilous lands thou sawest, sounding shores

And seas and forests drear, island and dale

And mountain dark. For thou with Tristram rod'st

Or Bedevere, in farthest Lyonesse.

Thou hadst a booth in Samarcand, whereat

Side-looking Magians trafficked; thence, by night,

An Afreet snatched thee, and with wings upbore

Beyond the Aral mount; or, hoping gain,

Thou, with a jar of money, didst embark,

For Balsorah, by sea. But chiefly thou

In that clear air took'st life; in Arcady

The haunted, land of song; and by the wells

Where most the gods frequent. There Chiron old,

In the Pelethronian antre, taught thee lore:

The plants, he taught, and by the shining stars

In forests dim to steer. There hast thou seen

Immortal Pan dance secret in a glade,

And, dancing, roll his eyes; these, where they fell,

Shed glee, and through the congregated oaks

A flying horror winged; while all the earth

To the god's pregnant footing thrilled within.

Or whiles, beside the sobbing stream, he breathed,

In his clutched pipe unformed and wizard strains

Divine yet brutal; which the forest heard,

And thou, with awe; and far upon the plain

The unthinking ploughman started and gave ear.

Now things there are that, upon him who sees,

A strong vocation lay; and strains there are

That whoso hears shall hear for evermore.

For evermore thou hear'st immortal Pan

And those melodious godheads, ever young

And ever quiring, on the mountains old.

What was this earth, child of the gods, to thee?

Forth from thy dreamland thou, a dreamer, cam'st

And in thine ears the olden music rang,

And in thy mind the doings of the dead,

And those heroic ages long forgot.

To a so fallen earth, alas! too late,

Alas! in evil days, thy steps return,

To list at noon for nightingales, to grow

A dweller on the beach till Argo come

That came long since, a lingerer by the pool

Where that desirèd angel bathes no more.

As when the Indian to Dakota comes,

Or farthest Idaho, and where he dwelt,

He with his clan, a humming city finds;

Thereon awhile, amazed, he stares, and then

To right and leftward, like a questing dog,

Seeks first the ancestral altars, then the hearth

Long cold with rains, and where old terror lodged,

And where the dead. So thee undying Hope,

With all her pack, hunts screaming through the years:

Here, there, thou fleeëst; but nor here nor there

The pleasant gods abide, the glory dwells.

That, that was not Apollo, not the god.

This was not Venus, though she Venus seemed

A moment. And though fair yon river move,

She, all the way, from disenchanted fount

To seas unhallowed runs; the gods forsook

Long since her trembling rushes; from her plains

Disconsolate, long since adventure fled;

And now although the inviting river flows,

And every poplared cape, and every bend

Or willowy islet, win upon thy soul

And to thy hopeful shallop whisper speed;

Yet hope not thou at all; hope is no more;

And O, long since the golden groves are dead

The faery cities vanished from the land!

XVI—TO W. E. HENLEY

The year runs through her phases; rain and sun,

Springtime and summer pass; winter succeeds;

But one pale season rules the house of death.

Cold falls the imprisoned daylight; fell disease

By each lean pallet squats, and pain and sleep

Toss gaping on the pillows.

      But O thou!

Uprise and take thy pipe. Bid music flow,

Strains by good thoughts attended, like the spring

The swallows follow over land and sea.

Pain sleeps at once; at once, with open eyes,

Dozing despair awakes. The shepherd sees

His flock come bleating home; the seaman hears
Once more the cordage rattle. Airs of home!
Youth, love and roses blossom; the gaunt ward
Dislimns and disappears, and, opening out,
Shows brooks and forests, and the blue beyond
Of mountains.
 Small the pipe; but oh! do thou,
Peak-faced and suffering piper, blow therein
The dirge of heroes dead; and to these sick,
These dying, sound the triumph over death.
Behold! each greatly breathes; each tastes a joy
Unknown before, in dying; for each knows
A hero dies with him—though unfulfilled,
Yet conquering truly—and not dies in vain

So is pain cheered, death comforted; the house
Of sorrow smiles to listen. Once again—
O thou, Orpheus and Heracles, the bard
And the deliverer, touch the stops again!

XVII—HENRY JAMES

Who comes to-night? We ope the doors in vain.
Who comes? My bursting walls, can you contain
The presences that now together throng

Your narrow entry, as with flowers and song,

As with the air of life, the breath of talk?

Lo, how these fair immaculate women walk

Behind their jocund maker; and we see

Slighted De Mauves, and that far different she,

Gressie, the trivial sphynx; and to our feast

Daisy and Barb and Chancellor (she not least!)

With all their silken, all their airy kin,

Do like unbidden angels enter in.

But he, attended by these shining names,

Comes (best of all) himself—our welcome James.

XVIII—THE MIRROR SPEAKS

Where the bells peal far at sea

Cunning fingers fashioned me.

There on palace walls I hung

While that Consuelo sung;

But I heard, though I listened well,

Never a note, never a trill,

Never a beat of the chiming bell.

There I hung and looked, and there

In my gray face, faces fair

Shone from under shining hair.

Well I saw the poising head,

But the lips moved and nothing said;

And when lights were in the hall,

Silent moved the dancers all.

So awhile I glowed, and then

Fell on dusty days and men;

Long I slumbered packed in straw,

Long I none but dealers saw;

Till before my silent eye

One that sees came passing by.

Now with an outlandish grace,

To the sparkling fire I face

In the blue room at Skerryvore;

Where I wait until the door

Open, and the Prince of Men,

Henry James, shall come again.

XIX—KATHARINE

We see you as we see a face

That trembles in a forest place

Upon the mirror of a pool

Forever quiet, clear and cool;

And in the wayward glass, appears

To hover between smiles and tears,

Elfin and human, airy and true,

And backed by the reflected blue.

XX—TO F. J. S.

I read, dear friend, in your dear face

Your life's tale told with perfect grace;

The river of your life, I trace

Up the sun-chequered, devious bed

To the far-distant fountain-head.

Not one quick beat of your warm heart,

Nor thought that came to you apart,

Pleasure nor pity, love nor pain

Nor sorrow, has gone by in vain;

But as some lone, wood-wandering child

Brings home with him at evening mild

The thorns and flowers of all the wild,

From your whole life, O fair and true

Your flowers and thorns you bring with you!

XXI—REQUIEM

Under the wide and starry sky,

Dig the grave and let me lie.

Glad did I live and gladly die,
    And I laid me down with a will.

This be the verse you grave for me:
Here he lies where he longed to be;
Home is the sailor, home from sea,
    And the hunter home from the hill.

XXII—THE CELESTIAL SURGEON

If I have faltered more or less

In my great task of happiness;

If I have moved among my race

And shown no glorious morning face;

If beams from happy human eyes

Have moved me not; if morning skies,

Books, and my food, and summer rain

Knocked on my sullen heart in vain:—

Lord, thy most pointed pleasure take

And stab my spirit broad awake;

Or, Lord, if too obdurate I,

Choose thou, before that spirit die,

A piercing pain, a killing sin,

And to my dead heart run them in!

XXIII—OUR LADY OF THE SNOWS

Out of the sun, out of the blast,

Out of the world, alone I passed

Across the moor and through the wood

To where the monastery stood.

There neither lute nor breathing fife,

Nor rumour of the world of life,

Nor confidences low and dear,

Shall strike the meditative ear.

Aloof, unhelpful, and unkind,

The prisoners of the iron mind,

Where nothing speaks except the hell

The unfraternal brothers dwell.

Poor passionate men, still clothed afresh

With agonising folds of flesh;

Whom the clear eyes solicit still

To some bold output of the will,

While fairy Fancy far before

And musing Memory-Hold-the-door

Now to heroic death invite

And now uncurtain fresh delight:

O, little boots it thus to dwell

On the remote unneighboured hill!

O to be up and doing, O
Unfearing and unshamed to go
In all the uproar and the press
About my human business!
My undissuaded heart I hear
Whisper courage in my ear.
With voiceless calls, the ancient earth
Summons me to a daily birth.

Thou, O my love, ye, O my friends—
The gist of life, the end of ends—
To laugh, to love, to live, to die,
Ye call me by the ear and eye!

Forth from the casemate, on the plain
Where honour has the world to gain,
Pour forth and bravely do your part,
O knights of the unshielded heart!
Forth and forever forward!—out
From prudent turret and redoubt,
And in the mellay charge amain,

To fall but yet to rise again!
Captive? ah, still, to honour bright,
A captive soldier of the right!
Or free and fighting, good with ill?
Unconquering but unconquered still!

And ye, O brethren, what if God,
When from Heav'n's top he spies abroad,
And sees on this tormented stage
The noble war of mankind rage:
What if his vivifying eye,
O monks, should pass your corner by?
For still the Lord is Lord of might;
In deeds, in deeds, he takes delight;
The plough, the spear, the laden barks,
The field, the founded city, marks;
He marks the smiler of the streets,
The singer upon garden seats;
He sees the climber in the rocks:
To him, the shepherd folds his flocks.
For those he loves that underprop
With daily virtues Heaven's top,
And bear the falling sky with ease,

Unfrowning caryatides.

Those he approves that ply the trade,

That rock the child, that wed the maid,

That with weak virtues, weaker hands,

Sow gladness on the peopled lands,

And still with laughter, song and shout,

Spin the great wheel of earth about.

But ye?—O ye who linger still

Here in your fortress on the hill,

With placid face, with tranquil breath,

The unsought volunteers of death,

Our cheerful General on high

With careless looks may pass you by.

XXIV

Not yet, my soul, these friendly fields desert,

Where thou with grass, and rivers, and the breeze,

And the bright face of day, thy dalliance hadst;

Where to thine ear first sang the enraptured birds;

Where love and thou that lasting bargain made.

The ship rides trimmed, and from the eternal shore

Thou hearest airy voices; but not yet

Depart, my soul, not yet awhile depart.

Freedom is far, rest far. Thou art with life

Too closely woven, nerve with nerve intwined;

Service still craving service, love for love,

Love for dear love, still suppliant with tears.

Alas, not yet thy human task is done!

A bond at birth is forged; a debt doth lie

Immortal on mortality. It grows—

By vast rebound it grows, unceasing growth;

Gift upon gift, alms upon alms, upreared,

From man, from God, from nature, till the soul

At that so huge indulgence stands amazed.

Leave not, my soul, the unfoughten field, nor leave

Thy debts dishonoured, nor thy place desert

Without due service rendered. For thy life,

Up, spirit, and defend that fort of clay,

Thy body, now beleaguered; whether soon

Or late she fall; whether to-day thy friends

Bewail thee dead, or, after years, a man

Grown old in honour and the friend of peace.

Contend, my soul, for moments and for hours;

Each is with service pregnant; each reclaimed

Is as a kingdom conquered, where to reign.

As when a captain rallies to the fight

His scattered legions, and beats ruin back,

He, on the field, encamps, well pleased in mind.

Yet surely him shall fortune overtake,

Him smite in turn, headlong his ensigns drive;

And that dear land, now safe, to-morrow fall.

But he, unthinking, in the present good

Solely delights, and all the camps rejoice.

XXV

It is not yours, O mother, to complain,

Not, mother, yours to weep,

Though nevermore your son again

Shall to your bosom creep,

Though nevermore again you watch your baby sleep.

Though in the greener paths of earth,

Mother and child, no more

We wander; and no more the birth

Of me whom once you bore,

Seems still the brave reward that once it seemed of yore;

Though as all passes, day and night,

The seasons and the years,

From you, O mother, this delight,

This also disappears—

Some profit yet survives of all your pangs and tears.

The child, the seed, the grain of corn,

The acorn on the hill,

Each for some separate end is born

In season fit, and still

Each must in strength arise to work the almighty will.

So from the hearth the children flee,

By that almighty hand

Austerely led; so one by sea

Goes forth, and one by land;

Nor aught of all man's sons escapes from that command

So from the sally each obeys

The unseen almighty nod;

So till the ending all their ways

Blindfolded loth have trod:

Nor knew their task at all, but were the tools of God.

And as the fervent smith of yore
Beat out the glowing blade,
Nor wielded in the front of war
The weapons that he made,
But in the tower at home still plied his ringing trade;

So like a sword the son shall roam
On nobler missions sent;
And as the smith remained at home
In peaceful turret pent,
So sits the while at home the mother well content.

XXVI—THE SICK CHILD

Child. O mother, lay your hand on my brow!
O mother, mother, where am I now?
Why is the room so gaunt and great?
Why am I lying awake so late?

Mother. Fear not at all: the night is still.
Nothing is here that means you ill—
Nothing but lamps the whole town through,
And never a child awake but you.

Child. Mother, mother, speak low in my ear,
Some of the things are so great and near,
Some are so small and far away,
I have a fear that I cannot say,
What have I done, and what do I fear,
And why are you crying, mother dear?

Mother. Out in the city, sounds begin
Thank the kind God, the carts come in!
An hour or two more, and God is so kind,
The day shall be blue in the window-blind,
Then shall my child go sweetly asleep,
And dream of the birds and the hills of sheep.

XXVII—IN MEMORIAM F. A. S.

Yet, O stricken heart, remember, O remember
   How of human days he lived the better part.
April came to bloom and never dim December
   Breathed its killing chills upon the head or heart.

Doomed to know not Winter, only Spring, a being
   Trod the flowery April blithely for a while,
Took his fill of music, joy of thought and seeing,

Came and stayed and went, nor ever ceased to smile.

Came and stayed and went, and now when all is finished,
   You alone have crossed the melancholy stream,
Yours the pang, but his, O his, the undiminished
   Undecaying gladness, undeparted dream.

All that life contains of torture, toil, and treason,
   Shame, dishonour, death, to him were but a name.
Here, a boy, he dwelt through all the singing season
   And ere the day of sorrow departed as he came.

Davos, 1881.

XXVIII—TO MY FATHER

Peace and her huge invasion to these shores
Puts daily home; innumerable sails
Dawn on the far horizon and draw near;
Innumerable loves, uncounted hopes
To our wild coasts, not darkling now, approach:
Not now obscure, since thou and thine are there,
And bright on the lone isle, the foundered reef,
The long, resounding foreland, Pharos stands.

These are thy works, O father, these thy crown;

Whether on high the air be pure, they shine
Along the yellowing sunset, and all night
Among the unnumbered stars of God they shine;
Or whether fogs arise and far and wide
The low sea-level drown—each finds a tongue
And all night long the tolling bell resounds:
So shine, so toll, till night be overpast,
Till the stars vanish, till the sun return,
And in the haven rides the fleet secure.

In the first hour, the seaman in his skiff
Moves through the unmoving bay, to where the town
Its earliest smoke into the air upbreathes
And the rough hazels climb along the beach.
To the tugg'd oar the distant echo speaks.
The ship lies resting, where by reef and roost
Thou and thy lights have led her like a child.

This hast thou done, and I—can I be base?
I must arise, O father, and to port
Some lost, complaining seaman pilot home.

XXIX—IN THE STATES

With half a heart I wander here

  As from an age gone by
A brother—yet though young in years.
  An elder brother, I.

You speak another tongue than mine,
  Though both were English born.
I towards the night of time decline,
  You mount into the morn.

Youth shall grow great and strong and free,
  But age must still decay:
To-morrow for the States—for me,
  England and Yesterday.

San Francisco.

XXX—A PORTRAIT

I am a kind of farthing dip,
  Unfriendly to the nose and eyes;
A blue-behinded ape, I skip
  Upon the trees of Paradise.

At mankind's feast, I take my place
  In solemn, sanctimonious state,

And have the air of saying grace
   While I defile the dinner plate.

I am "the smiler with the knife,"
   The battener upon garbage, I—
Dear Heaven, with such a rancid life,
   Were it not better far to die?

Yet still, about the human pale,
   I love to scamper, love to race,
To swing by my irreverent tail
   All over the most holy place;

And when at length, some golden day,
   The unfailing sportsman, aiming at,
Shall bag, me—all the world shall say:
   Thank God, and there's an end of that!

XXXI

Sing clearlier, Muse, or evermore be still,
Sing truer or no longer sing!
No more the voice of melancholy Jacques
To wake a weeping echo in the hill;
But as the boy, the pirate of the spring,

From the green elm a living linnet takes,

One natural verse recapture—then be still.

XXXII—A CAMP [66]

The bed was made, the room was fit,

By punctual eve the stars were lit;

The air was still, the water ran,

No need was there for maid or man,

When we put up, my ass and I,

At God's green caravanserai.

XXXIII—THE COUNTRY OF THE CAMISARDS [67]

We travelled in the print of olden wars,

   Yet all the land was green,

   And love we found, and peace,

   Where fire and war had been.

They pass and smile, the children of the sword—

   No more the sword they wield;

   And O, how deep the corn

   Along the battlefield!

XXXIV—SKERRYVORE

For love of lovely words, and for the sake

Of those, my kinsmen and my countrymen,

Who early and late in the windy ocean toiled

To plant a star for seamen, where was then

The surfy haunt of seals and cormorants:

I, on the lintel of this cot, inscribe

The name of a strong tower.

XXXV—SKERRYVORE: The Parallel

Here all is sunny, and when the truant gull

Skims the green level of the lawn, his wing

Dispetals roses; here the house is framed

Of kneaded brick and the plumed mountain pine,

Such clay as artists fashion and such wood

As the tree-climbing urchin breaks. But there

Eternal granite hewn from the living isle

And dowelled with brute iron, rears a tower

That from its wet foundation to its crown

Of glittering glass, stands, in the sweep of winds,

Immovable, immortal, eminent.

XXXVI

My house, I say. But hark to the sunny doves

That make my roof the arena of their loves,

That gyre about the gable all day long

And fill the chimneys with their murmurous song:
Our house, they say; and mine, the cat declares
And spreads his golden fleece upon the chairs;
And mine the dog, and rises stiff with wrath
If any alien foot profane the path.
So too the buck that trimmed my terraces,
Our whilome gardener, called the garden his;
Who now, deposed, surveys my plain abode
And his late kingdom, only from the road.

XXXVII

My body which my dungeon is,
And yet my parks and palaces:—
   Which is so great that there I go
All the day long to and fro,
And when the night begins to fall
Throw down my bed and sleep, while all
The building hums with wakefulness—
Even as a child of savages
When evening takes her on her way,
(She having roamed a summer's day
Along the mountain-sides and scalp)
Sleeps in an antre of that alp:—
   Which is so broad and high that there,

As in the topless fields of air,

My fancy soars like to a kite

And faints in the blue infinite:—

   Which is so strong, my strongest throes

And the rough world's besieging blows

Not break it, and so weak withal,

Death ebbs and flows in its loose wall

As the green sea in fishers' nets,

And tops its topmost parapets:—

   Which is so wholly mine that I

Can wield its whole artillery,

And mine so little, that my soul

Dwells in perpetual control,

And I but think and speak and do

As my dead fathers move me to:—

   If this born body of my bones

The beggared soul so barely owns,

What money passed from hand to hand,

What creeping custom of the land,

What deed of author or assign,

Can make a house a thing of mine?

XXXVIII

Say not of me that weakly I declined

The labours of my sires, and fled the sea,

The towers we founded and the lamps we lit,

To play at home with paper like a child.

But rather say: In the afternoon of time

A strenuous family dusted from its hands

The sand of granite, and beholding far

Along the sounding coast its pyramids

And tall memorials catch the dying sun,

Smiled well content, and to this childish task

Around the fire addressed its evening hours.

BOOK II.—In Scots

TABLE OF COMMON SCOTTISH VOWEL SOUNDS

ae, ai	open A as in rare.
a', au, aw	AW as in law.
ea	open E as in mere, but this with exceptions, as heather = heather, wean = wain, lear = lair.
ee, ei, ie	open E as in mere.
oa	open O as in more.
ou	doubled O as in poor.
ow	OW as in bower.
u	doubled O as in poor.
ui or ü before R	(say roughly) open A as in rare.
ui or ü before any other consonant	(say roughly) close I as in grin.
y	open I as in kite.
i	pretty nearly what you please, much as in English, Heaven guide the reader through that labyrinth! But in Scots it dodges usually from the short I, as in grin, to the open E, as in mere. Find the blind, I may remark, are pronounced to rhyme with the preterite of grin.

I—THE MAKER TO POSTERITY

Far 'yont amang the years to be
When a' we think, an' a' we see,
An' a' we luve, 's been dung ajee
    By time's rouch shouther,
An' what was richt and wrang for me
    Lies mangled throu'ther,

It's possible—it's hardly mair—
That some ane, ripin' after lear—
Some auld professor or young heir,
    If still there's either—
May find an' read me, an' be sair
    Perplexed, puir brither!

"What tongue does your auld bookie speak?"
He'll spier; an' I, his mou to steik:
"No bein' fit to write in Greek,
    I write in Lallan,
Dear to my heart as the peat reek,
    Auld as Tantallon.

"Few spak it then, an' noo there's nane.
My puir auld sangs lie a' their lane,
Their sense, that aince was braw an' plain,
    Tint a'thegether,
Like runes upon a standin' stane
    Amang the heather.

"But think not you the brae to speel;
You, tae, maun chow the bitter peel;
For a' your lear, for a' your skeel,
    Ye're nane sae lucky;
An' things are mebbe waur than weel
    For you, my buckie.

"The hale concern (baith hens an' eggs,
Baith books an' writers, stars an' clegs)
Noo stachers upon lowsent legs
    An' wears awa';
The tack o' mankind, near the dregs,
    Rins unco law.

"Your book, that in some braw new tongue,
Ye wrote or prentit, preached or sung,

Will still be just a bairn, an' young
    In fame an' years,
Whan the hale planet's guts are dung
    About your ears;

"An' you, sair gruppin' to a spar
Or whammled wi' some bleezin' star,
Cryin' to ken whaur deil ye are,
    Hame, France, or Flanders—
Whang sindry like a railway car
    An' flie in danders."

II—ILLE TERRARUM

Frae nirly, nippin', Eas'lan' breeze,
Frae Norlan' snaw, an' haar o' seas,
Weel happit in your gairden trees,
    A bonny bit,
Atween the muckle Pentland's knees,
    Secure ye sit.

Beeches an' aiks entwine their theek,
An' firs, a stench, auld-farrant clique.
A' simmer day, your chimleys reek,
    Couthy and bien;

An' here an' there your windies keek

    Amang the green.

A pickle plats an' paths an' posies,

A wheen auld gillyflowers an' roses:

A ring o' wa's the hale encloses

    Frae sheep or men;

An' there the auld housie beeks an' dozes,

    A' by her lane.

The gairdner crooks his weary back

A' day in the pitaty-track,

Or mebbe stops awhile to crack

    Wi' Jane the cook,

Or at some buss, worm-eaten-black,

    To gie a look.

Frae the high hills the curlew ca's;

The sheep gang baaing by the wa's;

Or whiles a clan o' roosty craws

    Cangle thegether;

The wild bees seek the gairden raws,

    Weariet wi' heather.

Or in the gloamin' douce an' gray

The sweet-throat mavis tunes her lay;

The herd comes linkin' doun the brae;

    An' by degrees

The muckle siller müne maks way

    Amang the trees.

Here aft hae I, wi' sober heart,

For meditation sat apairt,

When orra loves or kittle art

    Perplexed my mind;

Here socht a balm for ilka smart

    O' humankind.

Here aft, weel neukit by my lane,

Wi' Horace, or perhaps Montaigne,

The mornin' hours hae come an' gane

    Abüne my heid—

I wadnae gi'en a chucky-stane

    For a' I'd read.

But noo the auld city, street by street,

An' winter fu' o' snaw an' sleet,

Awhile shut in my gangrel feet

    An' goavin' mettle;

Noo is the soopit ingle sweet,

    An' liltin' kettle.

An' noo the winter winds complain;

Cauld lies the glaur in ilka lane;

On draigled hizzie, tautit wean

    An' drucken lads,

In the mirk nicht, the winter rain

    Dribbles an' blads.

Whan bugles frae the Castle rock,

An' beaten drums wi' dowie shock,

Wauken, at cauld-rife sax o'clock,

    My chitterin' frame,

I mind me on the kintry cock,

    The kintry hame.

I mind me on yon bonny bield;

An' Fancy traivels far afield

To gaither a' that gairdens yield

    O' sun an' Simmer:
To hearten up a dowie chield,
    Fancy's the limmer!

III

When aince Aprile has fairly come,
An' birds may bigg in winter's lum,
An' pleisure's spreid for a' and some
    O' whatna state,
Love, wi' her auld recruitin' drum,
    Than taks the gate.

The heart plays dunt wi' main an' micht;
The lasses' een are a' sae bricht,
Their dresses are sae braw an' ticht,
    The bonny birdies!—
Puir winter virtue at the sicht
    Gangs heels ower hurdies.

An' aye as love frae land to land
Tirls the drum wi' eident hand,
A' men collect at her command,
    Toun-bred or land'art,
An' follow in a denty band

Her gaucy standart.

An' I, wha sang o' rain an' snaw,
An' weary winter weel awa',
Noo busk me in a jacket braw,
    An' tak my place
I' the ram-stam, harum-scarum raw,
    Wi' smilin' face.

IV—A MILE AN' A BITTOCK

A mile an' a bittock, a mile or twa,
Abüthe burn, ayont the law,
Davie an' Donal' an' Cherlie an' a',
    An' the müne was shinin' clearly!

Ane went hame wi' the ither, an' then
The ither went hame wi' the ither twa men,
An' baith wad return him the service again,
    An' the müne was shinin' clearly!

The clocks were chappin' in house an' ha',
Eleeven, twal an' ane an' twa;
An' the guidman's face was turnt to the wa',
    An' the müne was shinin' clearly!

A wind got up frae affa the sea,

It blew the stars as clear's could be,

It blew in the een of a' o' the three,

   An' the müne was shinin' clearly!

Noo, Davie was first to get sleep in his head,

"The best o' frien's maun twine," he said;

"I'm weariet, an' here I'm awa' to my bed."

   An' the müne was shinin' clearly!

Twa o' them walkin' an' crackin' their lane,

The mornin' licht cam gray an' plain,

An' the birds they yammert on stick an' stane,

   An' the müne was shinin' clearly!

O years ayont, O years awa',

My lads, ye'll mind whate'er befa'—

My lads, ye'll mind on the bield o' the law,

   When the müne was shinin' clearly.

V—A LOWDEN SABBATH MORN

The clinkum-clank o' Sabbath bells

Noo to the hoastin' rookery swells,

Noo faintin' laigh in shady dells,

    Sounds far an' near,

An' through the simmer kintry tells

    Its tale o' cheer.

An' noo, to that melodious play,

A' deidly awn the quiet sway—

A' ken their solemn holiday,

    Bestial an' human,

The singin' lintie on the brae,

    The restin' plou'man,

He, mair than a' the lave o' men,

His week completit joys to ken;

Half-dressed, he daunders out an' in,

    Perplext wi' leisure;

An' his raxt limbs he'll rax again

    Wi' painfü' pleesure.

The steerin' mither strang afit

Noo shoos the bairnies but a bit;

Noo cries them ben, their Sinday shüit

    To scart upon them,

Or sweeties in their pouch to pit,

    Wi' blessin's on them.

The lasses, clean frae tap to taes,

Are busked in crunklin' underclaes;

The gartened hose, the weel-filled stays,

    The nakit shift,

A' bleached on bonny greens for days,

    An' white's the drift.

An' noo to face the kirkward mile:

The guidman's hat o' dacent style,

The blackit shoon, we noo maun fyle

    As white's the miller:

A waefü' peety tae, to spile

    The warth o' siller.

Our Marg'et, aye sae keen to crack,

Douce-stappin' in the stoury track,

Her emeralt goun a' kiltit back

    Frae snawy coats,

White-ankled, leads the kirkward pack

    Wi' Dauvit Groats.

A thocht ahint, in runkled breeks,
A' spiled wi' lyin' by for weeks,
The guidman follows closs, an' cleiks
    The sonsie missis;
His sarious face at aince bespeaks
    The day that this is.

And aye an' while we nearer draw
To whaur the kirkton lies alaw,
Mair neebours, comin' saft an' slaw
    Frae here an' there,
The thicker thrang the gate an' caw
    The stour in air.

But hark! the bells frae nearer clang;
To rowst the slaw, their sides they bang;
An' see! black coats a'ready thrang
    The green kirkyaird;
And at the yett, the chestnuts spang
    That brocht the laird.

The solemn elders at the plate

Stand drinkin' deep the pride o' state:
The practised hands as gash an' great
    As Lords o' Session;
The later named, a wee thing blate
    In their expression.

The prentit stanes that mark the deid,
Wi' lengthened lip, the sarious read;
Syne wag a moraleesin' heid,
    An' then an' there
Their hirplin' practice an' their creed
    Try hard to square.

It's here our Merren lang has lain,
A wee bewast the table-stane;
An' yon's the grave o' Sandy Blane;
    An' further ower,
The mither's brithers, dacent men!
    Lie a' the fower.

Here the guidman sall bide awee
To dwall amang the deid; to see
Auld faces clear in fancy's e'e;

Belike to hear
Auld voices fa'in saft an' slee
　　　On fancy's ear.

Thus, on the day o' solemn things,
The bell that in the steeple swings
To fauld a scaittered faim'ly rings
　　　Its walcome screed;
An' just a wee thing nearer brings
　　　The quick an' deid.

But noo the bell is ringin' in;
To tak their places, folk begin;
The minister himsel' will shüne
　　　Be up the gate,
Filled fu' wi' clavers about sin
　　　An' man's estate.

The tünes are up—French, to be shüre,
The faithfü' French, an' twa-three mair;
The auld prezentor, hoastin' sair,
　　　Wales out the portions,
An' yirks the tüne into the air

Wi' queer contortions.

Follows the prayer, the readin' next,
An' than the fisslin' for the text—
The twa-three last to find it, vext
    But kind o' proud;
An' than the peppermints are raxed,
    An' southernwood.

For noo's the time whan pews are seen
Nid-noddin' like a mandareen;
When tenty mithers stap a preen
    In sleepin' weans;
An' nearly half the parochine
    Forget their pains.

There's just a waukrif' twa or three:
Thrawn commentautors sweer to 'gree,
Weans glowrin' at the bumlin' bee
    On windie-glasses,
Or lads that tak a keek a-glee
    At sonsie lasses.

Himsel', meanwhile, frae whaur he cocks

An' bobs belaw the soundin'-box,

The treesures of his words unlocks

    Wi' prodigality,

An' deals some unco dingin' knocks

    To infidality.

Wi' sappy unction, hoo he burkes

The hopes o' men that trust in works,

Expounds the fau'ts o' ither kirks,

    An' shaws the best o' them

No muckle better than mere Turks,

    When a's confessed o' them.

Bethankit! what a bonny creed!

What mair would ony Christian need?—

The braw words rumm'le ower his heid,

    Nor steer the sleeper;

And in their restin' graves, the deid

    Sleep aye the deeper.

Note.—It may be guessed by some that I had a certain parish in my eye, and this makes it proper I should add a word of disclamation. In my time there have been two ministers in that parish. Of the first I have a special reason to speak well, even had there been any to think ill. The second I have often met in private and long (in the due phrase) "sat under" in his church, and neither here nor there have I heard an unkind or ugly word upon his lips.

The preacher of the text had thus no original in that particular parish; but when I was a boy, he might have been observed in many others; he was then (like the schoolmaster) abroad; and by recent advices, it would seem he has not yet entirely disappeared.

VI—THE SPAEWIFE

O, I wad like to ken—to the beggar-wife says I—

Why chops are guid to brander and nane sae guid to fry.

An' siller, that's sae braw to keep, is brawer still to gi'e.

—It's gey an' easy spierin', says the beggar-wife to me.

O, I wad like to ken—to the beggar-wife says I—

Hoo a' things come to be whaur we find them when we try,

The lasses in their claes an' the fishes in the sea.

—It's gey an' easy spierin', says the beggar-wife to me.

O, I wad like to ken—to the beggar-wife says I—

Why lads are a' to sell an' lasses a' to buy;

An' naebody for dacency but barely twa or three

—It's gey an' easy spierin', says the beggar-wife to me.

O, I wad like to ken—to the beggar-wife says I—

Gin death's as shüre to men as killin' is to kye,

Why God has filled the yearth sae fu' o' tasty things to pree.

—It's gey an' easy spierin', says the beggar-wife to me.

O, I wad like to ken—to the beggar wife says I—

The reason o' the cause an' the wherefore o' the why,

Wi' mony anither riddle brings the tear into my e'e.

—It's gey an' easy spierin', says the beggar-wife to me.

VII—THE BLAST—1875

It's rainin'. Weet's the gairden sod,

Weet the lang roads whaur gangrels plod—

A maist unceevil thing o' God

    In mid July—

If ye'll just curse the sneckdraw, dod!

    An' sae wull I!

He's a braw place in Heev'n, ye ken,

An' lea's us puir, forjaskit men

Clamjamfried in the but and ben

    He ca's the earth—

A wee bit inconvenient den

    No muckle worth;

An' whiles, at orra times, keeks out,

Sees what puir mankind are about;

An' if He can, I've little doubt,

Upsets their plans;
He hates a' mankind, brainch and root,
    An' a' that's man's.

An' whiles, whan they tak heart again,
An' life i' the sun looks braw an' plain,
Doun comes a jaw o' droukin' rain
    Upon their honours—
God sends a spate outower the plain,
    Or mebbe thun'ers.

Lord safe us, life's an unco thing!
Simmer an' Winter, Yule an' Spring,
The damned, dour-heartit seasons bring
    A feck o' trouble.
I wadnae try't to be a king—
    No, nor for double.

But since we're in it, willy-nilly,
We maun be watchfü', wise an' skilly,
An' no mind ony ither billy,
    Lassie nor God.
But drink—that's my best counsel till 'e:
    Sae tak the nod.

VIII—THE COUNTERBLAST—1886

My bonny man, the warld, it's true,
Was made for neither me nor you;
It's just a place to warstle through,
    As job confessed o't;
And aye the best that we'll can do
    Is mak the best o't.

There's rowth o' wrang, I'm free to say:
The simmer brunt, the winter blae,
The face of earth a' fyled wi' clay
    An' dour wi' chuckies,
An' life a rough an' land'art play
    For country buckies.

An' food's anither name for clart;
An' beasts an' brambles bite an' scart;
An' what would WE be like, my heart!
    If bared o' claethin'?
—Aweel, I cannae mend your cart:
    It's that or naethin'.

A feck o' folk frae first to last

Have through this queer experience passed;
Twa-three, I ken, just damn an' blast
    The hale transaction;
But twa-three ithers, east an' wast,
    Fand satisfaction,

Whaur braid the briery muirs expand,
A waefu' an' a weary land,
The bumblebees, a gowden band,
    Are blithely hingin';
An' there the canty wanderer fand
    The laverock singin'.

Trout in the burn grow great as herr'n,
The simple sheep can find their fair'n';
The wind blaws clean about the cairn
    Wi' caller air;
The muircock an' the barefit bairn
    Are happy there.

Sic-like the howes o' life to some:
Green loans whaur they ne'er fash their thumb.
But mark the muckle winds that come

    Soopin' an' cool,
Or hear the powrin' burnie drum
    In the shilfa's pool.

The evil wi' the guid they tak;
They ca' a gray thing gray, no black;
To a steigh brae, a stubborn back
    Addressin' daily;
An' up the rude, unbieldy track
    O' life, gang gaily.

What you would like's a palace ha',
Or Sinday parlour dink an' braw
Wi' a' things ordered in a raw
    By denty leddies.
Weel, than, ye cannae hae't: that's a'
    That to be said is.

An' since at life ye've taen the grue,
An' winnae blithely hirsle through,
Ye've fund the very thing to do—
    That's to drink speerit;
An' shüne we'll hear the last o' you—

An' blithe to hear it!

The shoon ye coft, the life ye lead,
Ithers will heir when aince ye're deid;
They'll heir your tasteless bite o' breid,
    An' find it sappy;
They'll to your dulefü' house succeed,
    An' there be happy.

As whan a glum an' fractious wean
Has sat an' sullened by his lane
Till, wi' a rowstin' skelp, he's taen
    An' shoo'd to bed—
The ither bairns a' fa' to play'n',
    As gleg's a gled.

IX—THE COUNTERBLAST IRONICAL

It's strange that God should fash to frame
    The yearth and lift sae hie,
An' clean forget to explain the same
    To a gentleman like me.

They gutsy, donnered ither folk,
    Their weird they weel may dree;

But why present a pig in a poke
   To a gentleman like me?

They ither folk their parritch eat
   An' sup their sugared tea;
But the mind is no to be wyled wi' meat
   Wi' a gentleman like me.

They ither folk, they court their joes
   At gloamin' on the lea;
But they're made of a commoner clay, I suppose,
   Than a gentleman like me.

They ither folk, for richt or wrang,
   They suffer, bleed, or dee;
But a' thir things are an emp'y sang
   To a gentleman like me.

It's a different thing that I demand,
   Tho' humble as can be—
A statement fair in my Maker's hand
   To a gentleman like me:

A clear account writ fair an' broad,

An' a plain apologie;
Or the deevil a ceevil word to God
From a gentleman like me.

X—THEIR LAUREATE TO AN ACADEMY CLASS DINNER CLUB

Dear Thamson class, whaure'er I gang
It aye comes ower me wi' a spang:
"Lordsake! they Thamson lads—(deil hang
  Or else Lord mend them!)—
An' that wanchancy annual sang
  I ne'er can send them!"

Straucht, at the name, a trusty tyke,
My conscience girrs ahint the dyke;
Straucht on my hinderlands I fyke
  To find a rhyme t' ye;
Pleased—although mebbe no pleased-like—
  To gie my time t'ye.

"Weel," an' says you, wi' heavin' breist,
"Sae far, sae guid, but what's the neist?
Yearly we gaither to the feast,
  A' hopefu' men—
Yearly we skelloch 'Hang the beast—

Nae sang again!'"

My lads, an' what am I to say?
Ye shürely ken the Muse's way:
Yestreen, as gleg's a tyke—the day,
    Thrawn like a cuddy:
Her conduc', that to her's a play,
    Deith to a body.

Aft whan I sat an' made my mane,
Aft whan I laboured burd-alane
Fishin' for rhymes an' findin' nane,
    Or nane were fit for ye—
Ye judged me cauld's a chucky stane—
    No car'n' a bit for ye!

But saw ye ne'er some pingein' bairn
As weak as a pitaty-par'n'—
Less üsed wi' guidin' horse-shoe airn
    Than steerin' crowdie—
Packed aff his lane, by moss an' cairn,
    To ca' the howdie.

Wae's me, for the puir callant than!

He wambles like a poke o' bran,
An' the lowse rein, as hard's he can,
    Pu's, trem'lin' handit;
Till, blaff! upon his hinderlan'
    Behauld him landit.

Sic-like—I awn the weary fac'—
Whan on my muse the gate I tak,
An' see her gleed e'e raxin' back
    To keek ahint her;—
To me, the brig o' Heev'n gangs black
    As blackest winter.

"Lordsake! we're aff," thinks I, "but whaur?
On what abhorred an' whinny scaur,
Or whammled in what sea o' glaur,
    Will she desert me?
An' will she just disgrace? or waur—
    Will she no hurt me?"

Kittle the quaere! But at least
The day I've backed the fashious beast,
While she, wi' mony a spang an' reist,

>   Flang heels ower bonnet;
> An' a' triumphant—for your feast,
>   Hae! there's your sonnet!

XI—EMBRO HIE KIRK

The Lord Himsel' in former days
Waled out the proper tünes for praise
An' named the proper kind o' claes
    For folk to preach in:
Preceese and in the chief o' ways
    Important teachin'.

He ordered a' things late and air';
He ordered folk to stand at prayer,
(Although I cannae just mind where
    He gave the warnin',)
An' pit pomatum on their hair
    On Sabbath mornin'.

The hale o' life by His commands
Was ordered to a body's hands;
But see! this corpus juris stands
    By a' forgotten;
An' God's religion in a' lands

Is deid an' rotten.

While thus the lave o' mankind's lost,
O' Scotland still God maks His boast—
Puir Scotland, on whase barren coast
    A score or twa
Auld wives wi' mutches an' a hoast
    Still keep His law.

In Scotland, a wheen canty, plain,
Douce, kintry-leevin' folk retain
The Truth—or did so aince—alane
    Of a' men leevin';
An' noo just twa o' them remain—
    Just Begg an' Niven.

For noo, unfaithfü', to the Lord
Auld Scotland joins the rebel horde;
Her human hymn-books on the board
    She noo displays:
An' Embro Hie Kirk's been restored
    In popish ways.

O punctum temporis for action

To a' o' the reformin' faction,
If yet, by ony act or paction,
    Thocht, word, or sermon,
This dark an' damnable transaction
    Micht yet determine!

For see—as Doctor Begg explains—
Hoo easy 't's düne! a pickle weans,
Wha in the Hie Street gaither stanes
    By his instruction,
The uncovenantit, pentit panes
    Ding to destruction.

Up, Niven, or ower late—an' dash
Laigh in the glaur that carnal hash;
Let spires and pews wi' gran' stramash
    Thegether fa';
The rumlin' kist o' whustles smash
    In pieces sma'.

Noo choose ye out a walie hammer;
About the knottit buttress clam'er;
Alang the steep roof stoyt an' stammer,

A gate mis-chancy;
On the aul' spire, the bells' hie cha'mer,
    Dance your bit dancie.

Ding, devel, dunt, destroy, an' ruin,
Wi' carnal stanes the square bestrewin',
Till your loud chaps frae Kyle to Fruin,
    Frae Hell to Heeven,
Tell the guid wark that baith are doin'—
    Baith Begg an' Niven.

XII—THE SCOTSMAN'S RETURN FROM ABROAD

In a letter from Mr. Thomson to Mr. Johnstone.

In mony a foreign pairt I've been,
An' mony an unco ferlie seen,
Since, Mr. Johnstone, you and I
Last walkit upon Cocklerye.
Wi' gleg, observant een, I pass't
By sea an' land, through East an' Wast,
And still in ilka age an' station
Saw naething but abomination.
In thir uncovenantit lands
The gangrel Scot uplifts his hands

At lack of a' sectarian füsh'n,
An' cauld religious destitütion.
He rins, puir man, frae place to place,
Tries a' their graceless means o' grace,
Preacher on preacher, kirk on kirk—
This yin a stot an' thon a stirk—
A bletherin' clan, no warth a preen,
As bad as Smith of Aiberdeen!

At last, across the weary faem,
Frae far, outlandish pairts I came.
On ilka side o' me I fand
Fresh tokens o' my native land.
Wi' whatna joy I hailed them a'—
The hilltaps standin' raw by raw,
The public house, the Hielan' birks,
And a' the bonny U.P. kirks!
But maistly thee, the bluid o' Scots,
Frae Maidenkirk to John o' Grots,
The king o' drinks, as I conceive it,
Talisker, Isla, or Glenlivet!

For after years wi' a pockmantie

Frae Zanzibar to Alicante,

In mony a fash and sair affliction

I gie't as my sincere conviction—

Of a' their foreign tricks an' pliskies,

I maist abominate their whiskies.

Nae doot, themsel's, they ken it weel,

An' wi' a hash o' leemon peel,

And ice an' siccan filth, they ettle

The stawsome kind o' goo to settle;

Sic wersh apothecary's broos wi'

As Scotsmen scorn to fyle their moo's wi'.

An', man, I was a blithe hame-comer

Whan first I syndit out my rummer.

Ye should hae seen me then, wi' care

The less important pairts prepare;

Syne, weel contentit wi' it a',

Pour in the sperrits wi' a jaw!

I didnae drink, I didnae speak,—

I only snowkit up the reek.

I was sae pleased therein to paidle,

I sat an' plowtered wi' my ladle.

An' blithe was I, the morrow's morn,

To daunder through the stookit corn,

And after a' my strange mishanters,

Sit doun amang my ain dissenters.

An', man, it was a joy to me

The pu'pit an' the pews to see,

The pennies dirlin' in the plate,

The elders lookin' on in state;

An' 'mang the first, as it befell,

Wha should I see, sir, but yoursel'

I was, and I will no deny it,

At the first gliff a hantle tryit

To see yoursel' in sic a station—

It seemed a doubtfü' dispensation.

The feelin' was a mere digression;

For shüne I understood the session,

An' mindin' Aiken an' M'Neil,

I wondered they had düne sae weel.

I saw I had mysel' to blame;

For had I but remained at hame,

Aiblins—though no ava' deservin' 't—

They micht hae named your humble servant.

The kirk was filled, the door was steeked;

Up to the pu'pit ance I keeked;
I was mair pleased than I can tell—
It was the minister himsel'!
Proud, proud was I to see his face,
After sae lang awa' frae grace.

Pleased as I was, I'm no denyin'
Some maitters were not edifyin';
For first I fand—an' here was news!—
Mere hymn-books cockin' in the pews—
A humanised abomination,
Unfit for ony congregation.

Syne, while I still was on the tenter,
I scunnered at the new prezentor;
I thocht him gesterin' an' cauld—
A sair declension frae the auld.
Syne, as though a' the faith was wreckit,
The prayer was not what I'd exspeckit.
Himsel', as it appeared to me,
Was no the man he üsed to be.
But just as I was growin' vext
He waled a maist judeecious text,
An', launchin' into his prelections,
Swoopt, wi' a skirl, on a' defections.

O what a gale was on my speerit
To hear the p'ints o' doctrine clearit,
And a' the horrors o' damnation
Set furth wi' faithfu' ministration!
Nae shauchlin' testimony here—
We were a' damned, an' that was clear,
I owned, wi' gratitude an' wonder,
He was a pleasure to sit under.

XIII

Late in the nicht in bed I lay,
The winds were at their weary play,
An' tirlin' wa's an' skirlin' wae
    Through Heev'n they battered;—
On-ding o' hail, on-blaff o' spray,
    The tempest blattered.

The masoned house it dinled through;
It dung the ship, it cowped the coo'.
The rankit aiks it overthrew,
    Had braved a' weathers;
The strang sea-gleds it took an' blew
    Awa' like feathers.

The thrawes o' fear on a' were shed,

An' the hair rose, an' slumber fled,

An' lichts were lit an' prayers were said

    Through a' the kintry;

An' the cauld terror clum in bed

    Wi' a' an' sindry.

To hear in the pit-mirk on hie

The brangled collieshangie flie,

The warl', they thocht, wi' land an' sea,

    Itsel' wad cowpit;

An' for auld airn, the smashed debris

    By God be rowpit.

Meanwhile frae far Aldeboran,

To folks wi' talescopes in han',

O' ships that cowpit, winds that ran,

    Nae sign was seen,

But the wee warl' in sunshine span

    As bricht's a preen.

I, tae, by God's especial grace,

Dwall denty in a bieldy place,

Wi' hosened feet, wi' shaven face,

   Wi' dacent mainners:

A grand example to the race

   O' tautit sinners!

The wind may blaw, the heathen rage,

The deil may start on the rampage;—

The sick in bed, the thief in cage—

   What's a' to me?

Cosh in my house, a sober sage,

   I sit an' see.

An' whiles the bluid spangs to my bree,

To lie sae saft, to live sae free,

While better men maun do an' die

   In unco places.

"Whaur's God?" I cry, an' "Whae is me

   To hae sic graces?"

I mind the fecht the sailors keep,

But fire or can'le, rest or sleep,

In darkness an' the muckle deep;

An' mind beside

The herd that on the hills o' sheep

    Has wandered wide.

I mind me on the hoastin' weans—

The penny joes on causey stanes—

The auld folk wi' the crazy banes,

    Baith auld an' puir,

That aye maun thole the winds an' rains

    An' labour sair.

An' whiles I'm kind o' pleased a blink,

An' kind o' fleyed forby, to think,

For a' my rowth o' meat an' drink

    An' waste o' crumb,

I'll mebbe have to thole wi' skink

    In Kingdom Come.

For God whan jowes the Judgment bell,

Wi' His ain Hand, His Leevin' Sel',

Sall ryve the guid (as Prophets tell)

    Frae them that had it;

And in the reamin' pat o' Hell,

The rich be scaddit.

O Lord, if this indeed be sae,
Let daw that sair an' happy day!
Again' the warl', grawn auld an' gray,
    Up wi' your aixe!
An' let the puir enjoy their play—
    I'll thole my paiks.

XIV—MY CONSCIENCE!

Of a' the ills that flesh can fear,
The loss o' frien's, the lack o' gear,
A yowlin' tyke, a glandered mear,
    A lassie's nonsense—
There's just ae thing I cannae bear,
    An' that's my conscience.

Whan day (an' a' excüse) has gane,
An' wark is düne, and duty's plain,
An' to my chalmer a' my lane
    I creep apairt,
My conscience! hoo the yammerin' pain
    Stends to my heart!

A' day wi' various ends in view

The hairsts o' time I had to pu',

An' made a hash wad staw a soo,

    Let be a man!—

My conscience! whan my han's were fu',

    Whaur were ye than?

An' there were a' the lures o' life,

There pleesure skirlin' on the fife,

There anger, wi' the hotchin' knife

    Ground shairp in Hell—

My conscience!—you that's like a wife!—

    Whaur was yoursel'?

I ken it fine: just waitin' here,

To gar the evil waur appear,

To clart the guid, confuse the clear,

    Mis-ca' the great,

My conscience! an' to raise a steer

    Whan a's ower late.

Sic-like, some tyke grawn auld and blind,

Whan thieves brok' through the gear to p'ind,

Has lain his dozened length an' grinned

  At the disaster;
An' the morn's mornin', wud's the wind,
  Yokes on his master.

XV—TO DOCTOR JOHN BROWN

(Whan the dear doctor, dear to a',
Was still amang us here belaw,
I set my pipes his praise to blaw
  Wi' a' my speerit;
But noo, Dear Doctor! he's awa',
  An' ne'er can hear it.)

By Lyne and Tyne, by Thames and Tees,
By a' the various river-Dee's,
In Mars and Manors 'yont the seas
  Or here at hame,
Whaure'er there's kindly folk to please,
  They ken your name.

They ken your name, they ken your tyke,
They ken the honey from your byke;
But mebbe after a' your fyke,
  (The trüth to tell)
It's just your honest Rab they like,

An' no yoursel'.

As at the gowff, some canny play'r
Should tee a common ba' wi' care—
Should flourish and deleever fair
    His souple shintie—
An' the ba' rise into the air,
    A leevin' lintie:

Sae in the game we writers play,
There comes to some a bonny day,
When a dear ferlie shall repay
    Their years o' strife,
An' like your Rab, their things o' clay,
    Spreid wings o' life.

Ye scarce deserved it, I'm afraid—
You that had never learned the trade,
But just some idle mornin' strayed
    Into the schüle,
An' picked the fiddle up an' played
    Like Neil himsel'.

Your e'e was gleg, your fingers dink;

Ye didnae fash yoursel' to think,

But wove, as fast as puss can link,

    Your denty wab:—

Ye stapped your pen into the ink,

    An' there was Rab!

Sinsyne, whaure'er your fortune lay

By dowie den, by canty brae,

Simmer an' winter, nicht an' day,

    Rab was aye wi' ye;

An' a' the folk on a' the way

    Were blithe to see ye.

O sir, the gods are kind indeed,

An' hauld ye for an honoured heid,

That for a wee bit clarkit screed

    Sae weel reward ye,

An' lend—puir Rabbie bein' deid—

    His ghaist to guard ye.

For though, whaure'er yoursel' may be,

We've just to turn an' glisk a wee,

An' Rab at heel we're shüre to see

  Wi' gladsome caper:—
The bogle of a bogle, he—
  A ghaist o' paper!

And as the auld-farrand hero sees
In Hell a bogle Hercules,
Pit there the lesser deid to please,
  While he himsel'
Dwalls wi' the muckle gods at ease
  Far raised frae hell:

Sae the true Rabbie far has gane
On kindlier business o' his ain
Wi' aulder frien's; an' his breist-bane
  An' stumpie tailie,
He birstles at a new hearth stane
  By James and Ailie.

XVI

It's an owercome sooth for age an' youth
 And it brooks wi' nae denial,
That the dearest friends are the auldest friends
 And the young are just on trial.

There's a rival bauld wi' young an' auld
   And it's him that has bereft me;
For the sürest friends are the auldest friends
   And the maist o' mines hae left me.

There are kind hearts still, for friends to fill
   And fools to take and break them;
But the nearest friends are the auldest friends
   And the grave's the place to seek them.

Footnotes

[27] Life on the Lagoons, by H. F. Brown, originally burned in the fire at Messrs. Kegan Paul, Trench. and Co.'s.

[66] From Travels with a Donkey.

[67] From Travels with a Donkey.

About Author

Childhood and youth

Stevenson was born at 8 Howard Place, Edinburgh, Scotland on 13 November 1850 to Thomas Stevenson (1818–87), a leading lighthouse engineer, and his wife Margaret Isabella (born Balfour, 1829–97). He was christened Robert Lewis Balfour Stevenson. At about age 18, he changed the spelling of "Lewis" to "Louis", and he dropped "Balfour" in 1873.

Lighthouse design was the family's profession; Thomas's father (Robert's grandfather) was civil engineer Robert Stevenson, and Thomas's brothers (Robert's uncles) Alan and David were in the same field. Thomas's maternal grandfather Thomas Smith had been in the same profession. However, Robert's mother's family were gentry, tracing their lineage back to Alexander Balfour who had held the lands of Inchyra in Fife in the fifteenth century. His mother's father Lewis Balfour (1777–1860) was a minister of the Church of Scotland at nearby Colinton, and her siblings included physician George William Balfour and marine engineer James Balfour. Stevenson spent the greater part of his boyhood holidays in his maternal grandfather's house. "Now I often wonder what I inherited from this old minister," Stevenson wrote. "I must suppose, indeed, that he was fond of preaching sermons, and so am I, though I never heard it maintained that either of us loved to hear them."

Lewis Balfour and his daughter both had weak chests, so they often needed to stay in warmer climates for their health. Stevenson inherited a tendency to coughs and fevers, exacerbated when the family moved to a damp, chilly house at 1 Inverleith Terrace in 1851. The family moved again to the sunnier 17 Heriot Row when Stevenson was six years old, but the tendency to extreme sickness in winter remained with him until he was 11. Illness was a recurrent feature of his adult life and left him extraordinarily thin. Contemporaneous views were that he had tuberculosis, but more recent views are that it was bronchiectasis or even sarcoidosis.

Stevenson's parents were both devout Presbyterians, but the household was not strict in its adherence to Calvinist principles. His nurse Alison Cunningham (known as Cummy) was more fervently religious. Her mix of Calvinism and folk beliefs were an early source of nightmares for the child, and he showed a precocious concern for religion. But she also cared for him tenderly in illness, reading to him from John Bunyan and the Bible as he lay sick in bed and telling tales of the Covenanters. Stevenson recalled this time of sickness in "The Land of Counterpane" in A Child's Garden of Verses (1885), dedicating the book to his nurse.

Stevenson was an only child, both strange-looking and eccentric, and he found it hard to fit in when he was sent to a nearby school at age 6, a problem repeated at age 11 when he went on to the Edinburgh Academy; but he mixed well in lively games with his cousins in summer holidays at Colinton. His frequent illnesses often kept him away from his first school, so he was taught for long stretches by private tutors. He was a late reader, learning at age 7 or 8, but even before this he dictated stories to his mother and nurse, and he compulsively wrote stories throughout his childhood. His father was proud of this interest; he had also written stories in his spare time until his own father found them and told him to "give up such nonsense and mind your business." He paid for the printing of Robert's first publication at 16, entitled The Pentland Rising: A Page of History, 1666. It was an account of the Covenanters' rebellion which was published in 1866, the 200th anniversary of the event.

Education

In September 1857, Stevenson went to Mr Henderson's School in India Street, Edinburgh, but because of poor health stayed only a few weeks and did not return until October 1859. During his many absences he was taught by private tutors. In October 1861, he went to Edinburgh Academy, an independent school for boys, and stayed there sporadically for about fifteen months. In the autumn of 1863, he spent one term at an English boarding school at Spring Grove in Isleworth in Middlesex (now an urban area of West London). In October 1864, following an improvement to his health, he was sent to Robert Thomson's private school in Frederick Street, Edinburgh, where he remained until he went to university. In November 1867, Stevenson entered the University of Edinburgh to study engineering. He showed from the start no enthusiasm for his studies and devoted much energy to avoiding lectures. This time was more important for the friendships he made with other students in the Speculative Society (an exclusive debating club), particularly with Charles Baxter, who would become Stevenson's financial agent, and with a professor, Fleeming Jenkin, whose house staged amateur drama in which Stevenson took part, and whose biography he would later write. Perhaps most important at this point in his life was a cousin, Robert Alan Mowbray Stevenson (known as "Bob"), a lively and light-hearted young man who, instead of the family profession, had chosen to study art. Each year during vacations, Stevenson travelled to inspect the family's engineering works—to Anstruther and Wick in 1868, with his father on his official tour of Orkney and Shetland islands lighthouses in 1869, and for three weeks to the island of Erraid in 1870. He enjoyed the travels more for the material they gave for his writing than for any engineering interest. The voyage with his father pleased him because a similar journey of Walter Scott with Robert Stevenson had provided the inspiration for Scott's 1822 novel The Pirate. In April 1871, Stevenson notified his father of his decision to pursue a life of letters. Though the elder Stevenson was naturally disappointed, the surprise cannot have been great, and Stevenson's mother reported that he was "wonderfully resigned" to his son's choice. To provide some security, it was agreed that Stevenson should read Law (again at Edinburgh University) and be called to the Scottish bar. In his 1887 poetry collection Underwoods, Stevenson muses on his having turned from the family profession:

> *Say not of me that weakly I declined*
>
> *The labours of my sires, and fled the sea,*
>
> *The towers we founded and the lamps we lit,*
>
> *To play at home with paper like a child.*
>
> *But rather say: In the afternoon of time*

> *A strenuous family dusted from its hands*
> *The sand of granite, and beholding far*
> *Along the sounding coast its pyramids*
> *And tall memorials catch the dying sun,*
> *Smiled well content, and to this childish task*
> *Around the fire addressed its evening hours.*

In other respects too, Stevenson was moving away from his upbringing. His dress became more Bohemian; he already wore his hair long, but he now took to wearing a velveteen jacket and rarely attended parties in conventional evening dress. Within the limits of a strict allowance, he visited cheap pubs and brothels. More importantly, he had come to reject Christianity and declared himself an atheist. In January 1873, his father came across the constitution of the LJR (Liberty, Justice, Reverence) Club, of which Stevenson and his cousin Bob were members, which began: "Disregard everything our parents have taught us". Questioning his son about his beliefs, he discovered the truth, leading to a long period of dissension with both parents:

What a damned curse I am to my parents! As my father said "You have rendered my whole life a failure". As my mother said "This is the heaviest affliction that has ever befallen me". O Lord, what a pleasant thing it is to have damned the happiness of (probably) the only two people who care a damn about you in the world.

Early writing and travels

Stevenson was visiting a cousin in England in late 1873 when he met two people who became very important to him: Sidney Colvin and Fanny (Frances Jane) Sitwell. Sitwell was a 34-year-old woman with a son, who was separated from her husband. She attracted the devotion of many who met her, including Colvin, who married her in 1901. Stevenson was also drawn to her, and they kept up a warm correspondence over several years in which he wavered between the role of a suitor and a son (he addressed her as "Madonna"). Colvin became Stevenson's literary adviser and was the first editor of his letters after his death. He placed Stevenson's first paid contribution in The Portfolio, an essay entitled "Roads".

Stevenson was soon active in London literary life, becoming acquainted with many of the writers of the time, including Andrew Lang, Edmund Gosse, and Leslie Stephen, the editor of the Cornhill Magazine who took an interest in Stevenson's work. Stephen took Stevenson to visit a patient at the Edinburgh Infirmary named William Ernest Henley, an energetic and talkative man with a wooden leg. Henley became a close friend and occasional literary collaborator, until a quarrel broke up the friendship in 1888, and he is often considered to be the model for Long John Silver in Treasure Island.

Stevenson was sent to Menton on the French Riviera in November 1873 to recuperate after his health failed. He returned in better health in April 1874 and settled down to his studies, but he returned to France several times after that. He made long and frequent trips to the neighborhood of the Forest of Fontainebleau, staying at Barbizon, Grez-sur-Loing, and Nemours and becoming a member of the artists' colonies there. He also traveled to Paris to visit galleries and the theatres. He qualified for the Scottish bar in July 1875, and his father added a brass plate to the Heriot Row house reading "R.L. Stevenson, Advocate". His law studies did influence his books, but he never practised law; all his energies were spent in travel and writing. One of his journeys was a canoe voyage in Belgium and France with Sir Walter Simpson, a friend from the Speculative Society, a frequent travel companion, and the author of The Art of Golf (1887). This trip was the basis of his first travel book An Inland Voyage (1878).

Marriage

The canoe voyage with Simpson brought Stevenson to Grez in September 1876 where he met Fanny Van de Grift Osbourne (1840–1914), born in Indianapolis. She had married at age 17 and moved to Nevada to rejoin husband Samuel after his participation in the American Civil War. Their children were Isobel (or "Belle"), Lloyd, and Hervey (who died in 1875). But anger over her husband's infidelities led to a number of separations. In 1875, she had taken her children to France where she and Isobel studied art.

Stevenson returned to Britain shortly after this first meeting, but Fanny apparently remained in his thoughts, and he wrote the essay "On falling in love" for the Cornhill Magazine. They met again early in 1877 and became lovers. Stevenson spent much of the following year with her and her children in France. In August 1878, she returned to San Francisco and Stevenson remained in Europe, making the walking trip that formed the basis for Travels with a Donkey in the Cévennes (1879). But he set off to join her in August 1879, against the advice of his friends and without notifying his parents. He took second-class passage on the steamship Devonia, in part to save money but also to learn how others traveled and to increase the adventure of the journey. He then traveled overland by train from New York City to California. He later wrote about the experience in The Amateur Emigrant. It was good experience for his writing, but it broke his health.

He was near death when he arrived in Monterey, California, where some local ranchers nursed him back to health. He stayed for a time at the French Hotel located at 530 Houston Street, now a museum dedicated to his memory called the "Stevenson House". While there, he often dined "on the cuff," as he said, at a nearby restaurant run by Frenchman Jules Simoneau which stood at what is now Simoneau Plaza; several years later, he sent Simoneau an inscribed copy of his novel Strange Case of Dr Jekyll and Mr Hyde (1886), writing that it would be a stranger case still if Robert Louis Stevenson ever forgot Jules Simoneau. While in Monterey, he wrote an evocative article about "the Old Pacific Capital" of Monterey.

By December 1879, Stevenson had recovered his health enough to continue to San Francisco where he struggled "all alone on forty-five cents a day, and sometimes less, with quantities of hard work and many heavy thoughts," in an effort to support himself through his writing. But by the end of the winter, his health was broken again and he found himself at death's door. Fanny was now divorced and recovered from her own illness, and she came to his bedside and nursed him to recovery. "After a while," he wrote, "my spirit got up again in a divine frenzy, and has since kicked and spurred my vile body forward with great emphasis and success." When his father heard of his condition, he cabled him money to help him through this period.

Fanny and Robert were married in May 1880, although he said that he was "a mere complication of cough and bones, much fitter for an emblem of mortality than a bridegroom." He travelled with his new wife and her son Lloyd north of San Francisco to Napa Valley and spent a summer honeymoon at an abandoned mining camp on Mount Saint Helena. He wrote about this experience in The Silverado Squatters. He met Charles Warren Stoddard, co-editor of the Overland Monthly and author of South Sea Idylls, who urged Stevenson to travel to the South Pacific, an idea which returned to him many years later. In August 1880, he sailed with Fanny and Lloyd from New York to Britain and found his parents and his friend Sidney Colvin on the wharf at Liverpool, happy to see him return home. Gradually, his wife was able to patch up differences between father and son and make herself a part of the family through her charm and wit.

Attempted settlement in Europe and the US

Stevenson searched in vain between 1880 and 1887 for a residence suitable to his health. He spent his summers at various places in Scotland and England, including Westbourne, Dorset, a residential area in Bournemouth. It was during his time in Bournemouth that he wrote the story Strange Case of Dr Jekyll and Mr Hyde, naming the character Mr. Poole after the town of Poole which is situated next to Bournemouth. In Westbourne, he named his house Skerryvore after the tallest lighthouse in Scotland, which his uncle Alan had built (1838–44). In the wintertime, Stevenson travelled to France and lived at Davos Platz and the Chalet de Solitude at Hyères, where he was very happy for a time. "I have so many things to make life sweet for me," he wrote, "it seems a pity I cannot have that other one thing—health. But though you will be angry to hear it, I believe, for myself at least, what is is best." In spite of his ill health, he produced the bulk of his best-known work during these years. Treasure Island was published under the pseudonym "Captain George North" and became his first widely popular book; he wrote it during this time, along with Kidnapped, Strange Case of Dr Jekyll and Mr Hyde (which established his wider reputation), The Black Arrow: A Tale of the Two Roses, A Child's Garden of Verses, and Underwoods. He gave a copy of Kidnapped to his friend and frequent Skerryvore visitor Henry James.

His father died in 1887 and Stevenson felt free to follow the advice of his physician to try a complete change of climate, so he headed for Colorado with his mother and family. But after landing in New York, they decided to spend the winter in the Adirondacks at a cure cottage now known as Stevenson Cottage at Saranac Lake, New York. During the intensely cold winter, Stevenson wrote some of his best essays, including Pulvis et Umbra. He also began The Master of Ballantrae and lightheartedly planned a cruise to the southern Pacific Ocean for the following summer.

Politics

Stevenson believed in Conservatism for most of his life. His cousin and biographer Sir Graham Balfour said that "he probably throughout life would, if compelled to vote, have always supported the Conservative candidate." In 1866, Stevenson voted for Benjamin Disraeli, future Conservative Prime Minister of the United Kingdom, over Thomas Carlyle for the Lord Rectorship of the University of Edinburgh. During his college years, he briefly identified himself as a "red-hot socialist". He wrote at age 26: "I look back to the time when I was a Socialist with something like regret.... Now I know that in thus turning Conservative with years, I am going through the normal cycle of change and travelling in the common orbit of men's opinions."

Journey to the Pacific

In June 1888, Stevenson chartered the yacht Casco and set sail with his family from San Francisco. The vessel "plowed her path of snow across the empty deep, far from all track of commerce, far from any hand of help." The sea air and thrill of adventure for a time restored his health, and for nearly three years he wandered the eastern and central Pacific, stopping for extended stays at the Hawaiian Islands where he became a good friend of King Kalākaua. He befriended the king's niece Princess Victoria Kaiulani, who also had Scottish heritage. He spent time at the Gilbert Islands, Tahiti, New Zealand, and the Samoan Islands. During this period, he completed The Master of Ballantrae, composed two ballads based on the legends of the islanders, and wrote The Bottle Imp. He preserved the experience of these years in his various letters and in his In the South Seas (which was published posthumously). He made a voyage in 1889 with Lloyd on the trading schooner Equator, visiting Butaritari, Mariki, Apaiang, and Abemama in the Gilbert Islands. They spent several months on Abemama with tyrant-chief Tem Binoka, whom Stevenson described in In the South Seas.

Stevenson left Sydney on the Janet Nicoll in April 1890 for his third and final voyage among the South Seas islands. He intended to produce another book of travel writing to follow his earlier book In the South Seas, but it was his wife who eventually published her journal of their third voyage. (Fanny misnames the ship in her account The Cruise of the Janet Nichol.) A fellow passenger was Jack Buckland, whose stories of life as an island trader became the inspiration for the character of Tommy Hadden in The Wrecker (1892), which Stevenson and Lloyd Osbourne wrote together. Buckland visited the Stevensons at Vailima in 1894.

Last years

In 1890, Stevenson purchased a tract of about 400 acres (1.6 km^2) in Upolu, an island in Samoa where he established himself on his estate in the village of Vailima after two aborted attempts to visit Scotland. He took the native name Tusitala (Samoan for "Teller of Tales"). His influence spread among the Samoans, who consulted him for advice, and he soon became involved in local politics. He was convinced that the European officials who had been appointed to rule the Samoans were incompetent, and he published A Footnote to History after many futile attempts to resolve the matter. This was such a stinging protest against existing conditions that it resulted in the recall of two officials, and Stevenson feared for a time that it would result in his own deportation. He wrote to Colvin, "I used to think meanly of the plumber; but how he shines beside the politician!"

He also found time to work at his writing, although he felt that "there was never any man had so many irons in the fire". He wrote The Beach of Falesa, Catriona (titled David Balfour in the US), The Ebb-Tide, and the Vailima Letters during this period.

Stevenson grew depressed and wondered if he had exhausted his creative vein, as he had been "overworked bitterly" and that the best he could write was "ditch-water". He even feared that he might again become a helpless invalid. He rebelled against this idea: "I wish to die in my boots; no more Land of Counterpane for me. To be drowned, to be shot, to be thrown from a horse — ay, to be hanged, rather than pass again through that slow dissolution." He then suddenly had a return of energy and he began work on Weir of Hermiston. "It's so good that it frightens me," he is reported to have exclaimed. He felt that this was the best work he had done.

On 3 December 1894, Stevenson was talking to his wife and straining to open a bottle of wine when he suddenly exclaimed, "What's that?", asked his wife "does my face look strange?", and collapsed. He died within a few hours, probably of a cerebral haemorrhage. He was 44 years old. The Samoans insisted on surrounding his body with a watch-guard during the night and on bearing him on their shoulders to nearby Mount Vaea, where they buried him on a spot overlooking the sea on land donated by British Acting Vice Consul Thomas Trood. Stevenson had always wanted his Requiem inscribed on his tomb:

Under the wide and starry sky,

Dig the grave and let me lie.

Glad did I live and gladly die,

And I laid me down with a will.

This be the verse you grave for me:

Here he lies where he longed to be;

Home is the sailor, home from sea,

And the hunter home from the hill.

Stevenson was loved by the Samoans, and his tombstone epigraph was translated to a Samoan song of grief. (Source: Wikipedia)

CPSIA information can be obtained
at www.ICGtesting.com
Printed in the USA
BVHW031636160719
553580BV00003B/448/P